Gladys

Flash Harry

Martha

ALBERT

Gl

WHEN THE
THE MICE

LIONEL

MARTHA'S ~~CATS~~ AWAY WILL PLAY

Bruce Ingman

CANDLEWICK PRESS

When you go off to school,
you think I just sleep all day.
WELL, BOY,
HAVE I GOT NEWS
FOR YOU!

I have my own newspaper delivered to keep myself up-to-date with the goings-on in the cat world.

I keep myself fit to make sure that the dog next door can't catch me.

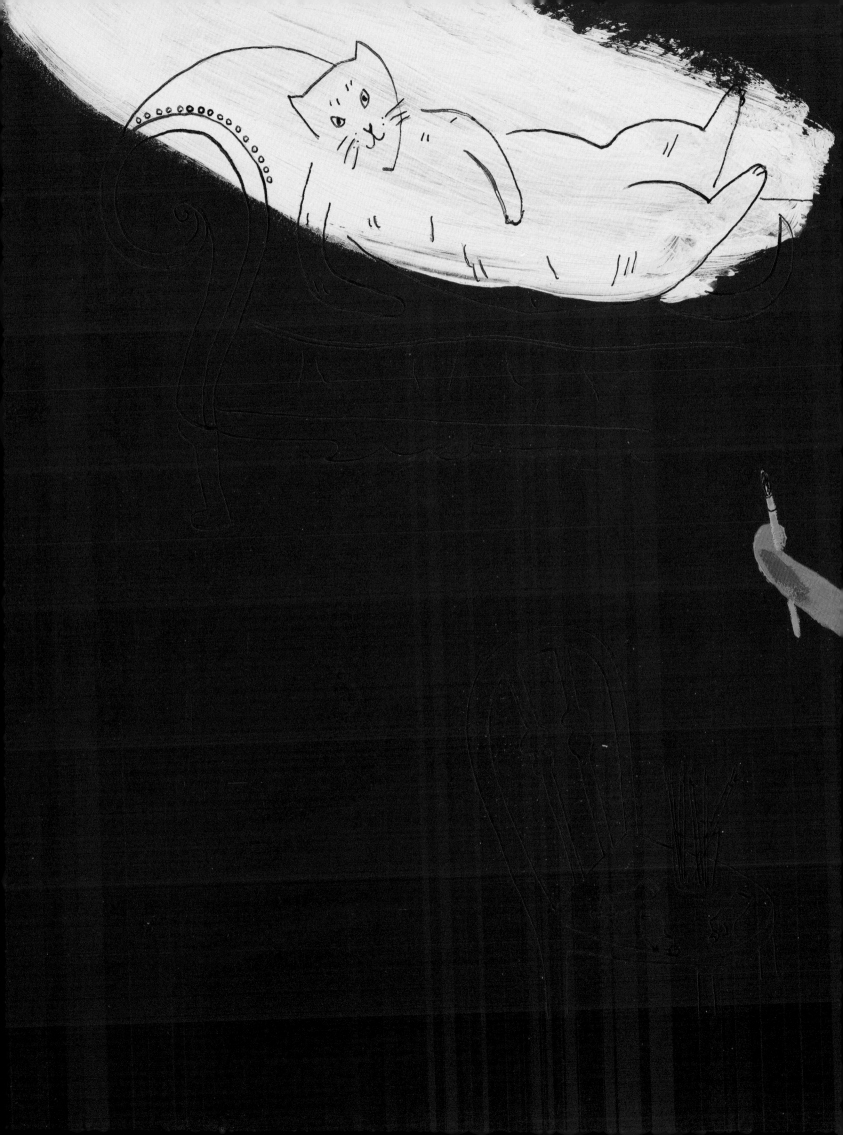

At ten o'clock I set up my easel and paints and *Gladys* from apartment #34 stops by to pose for me.

I cook myself some lunch. My favorite is a nice bit of salmon washed down with a cool saucer of milk.

I like to watch cartoons
while I eat my lunch.

I call my cousin **ALBERT**
in Atlantic City for a chat.

Sometimes in the afternoon Flash Harry knocks on the back door with his suitcase full of goodies.

I have a little nap, and—WOW—
do I have some good dreams.

I listen to the radio. I like the gardening programs that tell me all about the plants and flowers in our yard.

Then I go upstairs to get changed for my afternoon performance.

Cats come from far and near
to hear me play.

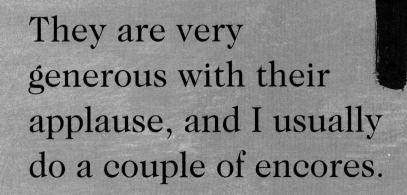

They are very
generous with their
applause, and I usually
do a couple of encores.

Sometimes I play with your toys.
Audrey from across the road
comes over quite often to play doctor.

If there's any time left, I take the car
for a quick spin around your room.

When I hear the gate, I dash downstairs to the sofa and pretend to be in the Land of Nod. Then you come in and kiss me hello, thinking I have been asleep all day.

Well, now you know!

This book is especially for Jessie

First Candlewick Press edition 2011

Library of Congress Cataloging-in-Publication Data is available.
Library of Congress Catalog Card Number pending

ISBN 978-0-7636-5135-0

10 11 12 13 14 15 SCP 10 9 8 7 6 5 4 3 2 1

Printed in Humen, Dongguan, China

This book was typeset in Caslon 224.
The illustrations were done in acrylic paint.

Candlewick Press
99 Dover Street
Somerville, Massachusetts 02144

visit us at www.candlewick.com

ALBERT

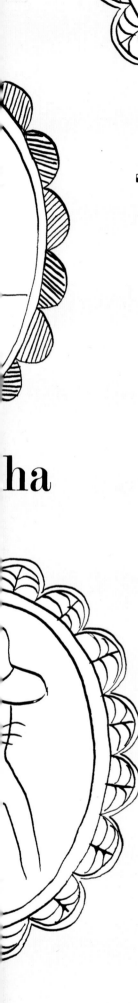

ha

Audrey

Flash Harry

Martha